The Convent School,

or
Early Experiences of a
Young Flagellant.

Restored Edition

Rosa Belinda Coote
1898

Dante Remy
Forward

Copyright 2025 by Black Fern

An Imprint of Erosetti Press

ISBN 978-1-968703-17-2

All Rights Reserved - Inquiries:
erosettipress.com

An imprint of ErosettiPress.com

The Convent School,

or
Early Experiences of a
Young Flagellant.

Restored Edition

Rosa Belinda Coote
1898

Dante Remy
Forward

"Between power and submission, pleasure and pain, desire and fulfillment, lies the true essence, of our erotic selves." —Forward, Dante Remy

Contents

Forward

I rubbed on to increase the pleasurable emotions which I felt driving me to strive and obtain, I knew not what. The frenzy now threw me into such a state of excitement that my fingers were plunged as far as possible up my virgin cunny, as I gasped, writhed, and tossed my bottom up and down. The crisis came at last, and my furious efforts were rewarded...

When *The Convent School* was first published in 1898, it sent shockwaves through Victorian society. Written by Rosa Belinda Coote (a pseudonym for William Lazenby, an English publisher and author who was active in the late 19th century) this provocative and unapologetically explicit tale was more than just a work of erotica—it was a bold challenge to the rigid moral codes of the time. For over a century, this story has continued to captivate readers, not just for its sensual content, but for its daring exploration of power dynamics, sexuality, and the darker sides of human desire. Now, with the release of *The Convent School: The Restored Edition*, complete with this contemporary, original decorative illustrations, and additional period erotic illustrations, we have the chance to revisit this seminal work and examine its lasting impact on the genre of erotic literature.

At the time of its release, *The Convent School* was privately printed, a common practice for works that skirted the boundaries of acceptability. Its full title included the byline *", or The Experiences of a Young Flagellant,"* projecting themes of bondage, discipline, and sadomasochism to potential readers.

Victorian society was outwardly conservative, with strict rules governing not just public behavior but the very thoughts and desires that people were allowed to entertain. Against this backdrop, *The Convent School* emerged as a stark and unflinching examination of the very taboos society sought to suppress.

The story of Lucille's journey explores five central themes of eroticism, each deeply intertwined with the psycho-sexual dynamics that underlie human desire. These themes—discipline and submission, the power of the forbidden, the awakening of sexual identity, the intersection of pain and pleasure, and the subversion of authority—create a narrative that is as much about psychological exploration as it is about physical encounters.

The first theme, **discipline and submission**, is the most overtly explored throughout the story. The ritualistic use of corporal punishment in the convent and under the guidance of figures like Miss Birch reveals a complex interplay between power and submission. Lucille's experience of being "stripped of every thing but my skirts and drawers" and tied up for punishment exemplifies how discipline becomes a means of controlling and shaping desire. The psycho-sexual underpinnings of this theme are rooted in the association of punishment with arousal, where the anticipation of pain becomes a conduit for pleasure. Lucille's submission is both enforced and internalized, reflecting the psychological process where control is both relinquished and desired.

The **power of the forbidden** is another key theme, driving the narrative's exploration of taboo and repression. The convent, a place of supposed sanctity, becomes the setting for the most illicit acts, where "the sight of my sufferings" is relished by those who wield power. The psycho-sexual charge of the forbidden is linked to the allure of what is socially or morally off-limits. The forbidden acts within the convent walls—clandestine sexual encounters, enforced punishments—create an erotic tension that is magnified by the very nature of their secrecy. The thrill of crossing boundaries, of engaging in what is expressly forbidden, heightens the erotic charge of these encounters.

Lucille's journey through the **awakening of sexual identity** is another significant theme. Her experiences, from her early encounters with Miss Birch to the complex dynamics with the Lady Superior, lead her to discover and embrace her own sexuality. Lucille's realization that "the drawers were unbuttoned and I could feel they were quite pulled down my thighs exposing the entire surface of my smarting rump" signals a moment of self-awareness, where pain and exposure are linked to a deeper understanding of her desires. This theme reflects the psycho-sexual process of discovering one's sexual identity through the exploration of power, submission, and the body's responses to these dynamics.

The **intersection of pain and pleasure** is a theme that runs through every encounter in the story. The narrative vividly depicts how pain, far from being purely negative, becomes a source of intense pleasure for Lucille. The stinging cuts of the birch rod, the humiliation of exposure, and the intense physical sensations all serve to blur the lines between pain and pleasure. This theme speaks to the psycho-sexual complexity of masochism, where pain is not only endured but transformed into a source of erotic pleasure. Lucille's exclamation, "Ah! You little wretch. Scream away!" as she is punished, reveals the entwining of agony and ecstasy, a central tenet of the story's eroticism.

Finally, the **subversion of authority** emerges as a powerful theme, where those in positions of power—Miss Birch, the Lady Superior, and even Lucille's father—use their authority to fulfill their own desires under the guise of discipline and morality. The psycho-sexual dynamics of this theme involve the eroticization of power, where authority figures derive pleasure from the act of controlling and dominating others. Lucille's experiences in the convent, where the Lady Superior "flew at me like a tigress" when denied her sexual advances, illustrate how authority is subverted to serve personal, often illicit, desires. This theme is a commentary on the corrupting influence of power and its ability to pervert even the most sacred institutions.

In one of the most telling quotes from the story, Lucille reflects on her experiences:

> I was choked and remember no more except that on recovering consciousness, the supposed Confessor Francisco was dressed as a gentleman, and I immediately recognized him as my husband as at the same instant he exclaimed, "Woman, my revenge is complete."

This moment of brutal revelation encapsulates the depth of betrayal and the perverse intertwining of power, control, and sexuality that defines her tragic journey. *Lucille's suffering is not just physical but deeply psychological,* as those she once trusted manipulate her vulnerabilities, turning what should be acts of care into acts of domination and degradation.

The psycho-sexual underpinnings of these themes suggest a deep exploration of the ways in which power, pain, and forbidden desires shape our understanding of sexuality. In *The Convent School,* the eroticism is not merely in the explicit acts but in the complex psychological dynamics at play—the way power is wielded, how submission is navigated, and the manner in which forbidden desires are both feared and embraced. The story forces readers to confront the uncomfortable truth that within the confines of societal repression, desire often finds expression in the most twisted and unexpected ways.

The Convent School remains a powerful exploration of eroticism because it taps into the primal aspects of human sexuality—the mingling of pleasure and pain, the allure of the forbidden, and the irresistible draw of power dynamics. These themes, though rooted in the context of a repressive Victorian society, resonate just as strongly today, as they speak to the universal and timeless aspects of human desire.

As we reflect on the legacy of *The Convent School*, we are reminded of the words Lucille speaks in her darkest moments: "What intense delight the sight of your agony is to us." It is a stark reminder of the dangers inherent in the abuse of power, and the ways in which society's most rigid structures can be the breeding grounds for its darkest desires. This restored edition invites readers not only to experience the raw eroticism of Lucille's journey but also to ponder the enduring questions it raises about the nature of desire, control, and the human psyche. As a final meditation on the story of Lucille, I offer you, the reader, these words to consider:

Between power and submission,

Pleasure and pain,

Desire and fulfillment,

Lies the true essence,

Of our erotic selves.

Dante Remy

"What intense delight the sight of your agony is to us."

The Convent School

By Rosa Belinda Coote

Prologue

Salomon said, in accents mild,
Spare the rod and spoil the child;
Be they man or be they maid,
Whip and wallop 'em, Salomon said.

The dicta of the Wise Man concerning discipline have been the source of inexpressible dolour to children for very many centuries; and it has only been within the last sixty years that ferocity in the treatment of infants (I am speaking of English children, Jean Jacques Rousseau shamed the French out of the practice of beating their offspring, nearly a hundred years ago) has been gradually diminishing. In the eighteenth century the lot of the British juvenile was certainly a cruel one That admirable woman, the mother of the Wesleys, held that a child should be made to desist from crying and to "fear the rod" at the mature age of twelve months; and Miss Maria Semple, writing on education in 1812, tells a story of a lady who was educated in early years by a relative. "On a certain day in every week she received corporal chastisement. If she had committed faults, 'the punishment was due;' if she had not, she probably would in the week ensuing. At the distance of more than half-a-century, the memory of this person, who bore a public character of piety and virtue, was spoken of, and justly, with aversion by the person she had thus treated." Thus Miss Maria Semple.—"G. A. S.," in the *Illustrated London News.*

"On a certain day in every week she received
corporal chastisement."

Introductory Letter
of
The Authoress

MY DEAR NELLIE,—

Since writing you my confessions, in that series of letters which you flattered me by calling "most interesting facts, and deliciously voluptuous reading for lovers of the rod," the following curious narrative has been entrusted to my confidential keeping by a young Countess of my acquaintance; but as there are no secrets between us, and I think it may afford some little pleasure in the perusal, I hasten to copy it out for you, from notes which I made day by day at the bedside of the dear young creature, as she told the particulars to me, at my visits during her long and painful illness, now, I am afraid, close upon a fatal termination; and you may guess how grieved I am to think that, although I now reserve her name as a secret, too solemn to be entrusted, even to you, the stillness of the grave will soon do away with all necessity for such reticence. Should my confessions ever be printed after our time, this tale certainly ought to bear them company, either as prefix or addenda.

Believe me, dear Nellie,
Your ever affectionate friend,
Rosa Belinda Coote.

London, 10th January, 1825.

"I was gradually awakened to the discovery of some
most mysterious kind of understanding ..."

Chapter I.

The Early Life of Lucille

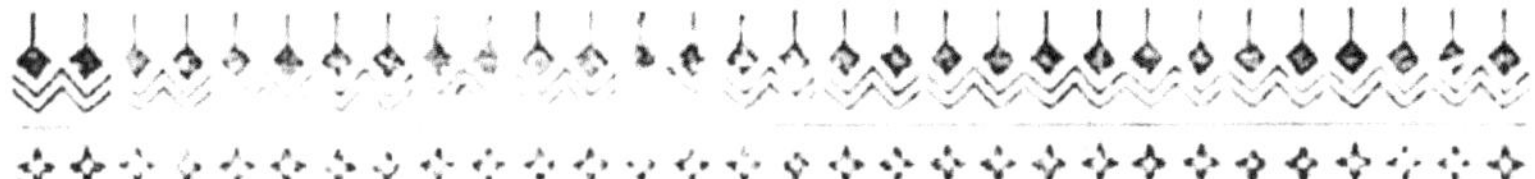

Since, dear Rosie, you are so interested to hear my birching and whipping experiences, I will try to recollect them as well as possible, but hope you will consider my weak state of health, and not press me to tell you too much at once.

Perhaps you do not know that almost from my infancy it was arranged that I should marry the Earl of Ellington, who was about twelve years my senior, being a family compact of a purely mercenary character, designed to consolidate some very doubtful title deeds, which now that our union has proved unfruitful, are likely to entail great expense and annoyance to our heirs-at-law.

My father, you know, was the Honourable Mr. Warton, and my mother died in giving birth to myself, so that I was brought up under a nurse, and afterwards, when about seven years old, a young lady was engaged as governess to instil my juvenile mind with the rudiments of learning, preparatory to being sent to a finishing school.

This lady's name was Miss Birch, and although my papa had known her father, Dr. Birch, for some years, I now believe that the fascination of her name had great influence with him in making a selection from the numerous, and in many instances more eligible ladies, who applied for the situation.

Miss Birch was a dark lady about thirty years of age when she entered our family, very good-looking, rather large pouting mouth, set off with lovely rows of most pearly white teeth, which, when she smiled or said much showed to beautiful effect in contrast to her rather swarthy complexion, dark brown eyes, and thick bushy black arching eyebrows, her figure was well moulded and plump, and being about five feet six, she had quite a commanding presence.

I was nearly eight years old before I began to notice the significant looks which occasionally passed between papa and governess, but hints were so often thrown out about the necessity of procuring a good birch rod for the naughty bottom of Lucille, that I was gradually awakened to the discovery of some most mysterious kind of understanding which must subsist between them. My infant brain was much puzzled and alarmed, as I already felt in imagination the tingling smart of the green twigs I so much dreaded.

Miss Birch seemed more exacting and severe over my lessons, especially when papa happened to be in the schoolroom, and now I will tell you my first experience of the rod.

One day after failing both in spelling and arithmetic she rang the bell and ordered the servant to request Mr. Warton's presence in the schoolroom for a few minutes. Papa entered with a very serious look, requesting Miss Birch to inform him of the cause of sending for him.

"Mr. Warton," said my governess, "you know we have had many serious conversations about the necessity for proper correction in case Miss Lucille should continue so inattentive to her studies, to-day she has failed in everything, and I am certain that unless her energies are sharpened up by the stinging smart of the rod she will go from bad to worse; I am so averse to wield the birch myself, and would much prefer that her papa should take in hand the serious whipping she ought to have."

"...lay her across your lap, Miss Birch, and pull up her clothes, whilst I get the rod out of the table drawer..."

Papa.—"Lucille, you hear what Miss Birch says, (I noticed him cast most excited and amorous looks towards the governess as he spoke), she has been most forbearing with you, and interceded with me many times to save your bottom, and even now cannot bring herself to lift her own hand to make you smart a little; it must indeed be a serious fault to induce her to ask me to use the rod, but, 'Spare the rod and spoil the child,' has always been a maxim with me; lay her across your lap, Miss Birch, and pull up her clothes, whilst I get the rod out of the table drawer." Miss Birch, with heaving bosom, and quite a deep blush upon her face.—"I feel as ashamed at baring her naughty posteriors as if I was going to suffer the degradation and humiliation myself, but come, Lucille dear, you must bear it, and I hope you will be a better and more diligent girl in future." Then catching me by the wrist, as I stood by her side covered with confusion, she tried to lay me across her knees, but I struggled and screamed, "No! No!! No!!! I won't be whipped! Oh! Oh!! dear papa, do forgive me this time!" my face quite crimson and streaming with tears. Papa, having got out the rod, a fine switch of long thin birch twigs, tied up with velvet and silk ribbons at the handle,—"Come! Come!! Lucille, this resistance will only make it worse for you." As he seized and threw me on the governess's lap, Miss Birch securing my head well under her left arm, speedily pulled up dress and skirts, till my fat little bottom was exposed in a tight fitting pair of drawers, my legs being left to kick about, although I was quite firmly secured, and to all intents quite helpless, and my toes could scarcely touch the ground.

I could hear papa whisking the birch about, and then he said, "That will do famously, Miss Birch, keep her head and shoulders well down as you hold up her skirts; much as I pity my darling little Lucille, I must do my duty and make her smart for her idleness in school."

My face was burning hot with the deep blushes of shame, and I struggled desperately to free my head from the vice-like pressure of Miss Birch's arm, as I begged with piteous sobs to be let off for this once. "Oh! dear papa! Oh! pray don't beat me!"

Papa.—"Indeed, I must, though every blow will send a pang to my own heart, you naughty, bad, inattentive girl, all this has come by your great idleness, and trusting too much to the kind heart of your governess." As he said this, three sharp stinging cuts whacked on my tight-fitting drawers in quick succession.

The pain was intense, I kicked, writhed and screamed for "Mercy! Mercy! Oh! Oh!! I will be good! Oh! Papa! Oh, Miss Birch, do let me go!"

Papa, in quite an excited tone, (for I could see nothing), "So you mean to be good in future! Do you feel the birch is doing you good already? Ha! ha!! my little Lucille, you must have a little more yet to make a perfect cure of your idleness." Whack—whack—whack—whack—four more cuts, each one more agonizing than the last, in spite of my sobbing and screaming. "Now, Miss Birch," he continued, "let her feel it on the bare flesh, open her drawers so we can see the effects of the cuts."

This was at once done, as I cried, "Ah! Ah!! No! No!! Oh, Papa! How cruel!"

Papa.—"What a sight. The rod has made her bottom blush finely. It's best to make her feel sore a few days, or she will soon forget it, and relapse into her old ways."

The drawers were unbuttoned, and I could feel they were quite pulled down my thighs, exposing the entire surface of my smarting rump, but I had only a few moments for reflection before the blows fell again in rapid succession, cutting, tearing, and scratching the skin, whilst the boiling blood in my veins seemed to throb as if it must spurt through the pores at every burning touch of the rod.

My head was pressed against the tumultuously heaving bosom of my governess, and notwithstanding the intensity of my suffering, I could plainly hear the beating of her heart, and knew that her thighs were tightly compressed together, whilst a strange tremor pervaded her entire frame.

"There, there, that will do," said Papa, in a very excited tone. "I've drawn the blood for her. Now, Miss Dunce, kneel and kiss the rod, and ask your kind governess to forgive you."

I slipped down on my knees, and hiding my face in my hands in her lap, promised Miss Birch "if she would forgive me now, to be a better girl in future."

"That will do. I don't want to be too hard upon Lucille this time. We will leave her to think over her disgrace and shame, and let her beware of the birch again," said Papa, taking Miss Birch's hand, to lead her from the room. "This has been a most agitating scene for your governess, who must repose in her private room for a while to recover herself."

The schoolroom door, which opened directly into her private room, was closed upon me, and the key turned in the lock, but all my hurts and bruises were insufficient to distract my attention from the peculiarly warm and excited glances which passed from papa towards my governess, whose face was suffused with blushes, and her eyes turned down, as if afraid to meet his ardent looks as they passed from the room.

My curiosity was excited so much, that I listened at the keyhole. Papa was evidently remaining in the governess's room. I could hear a rustling of her dress, as if some little struggle was taking place; a sound of smothered kisses, and soft expostulatory ejaculations, such as, "I dare not! Oh! No! No!! Not now! Pray leave me! Oh! Oh!!" Then an almost perfect quiet, except for a slight rustling sound, and, now and then, broken sighs with heavy breathing.

At last all was quiet, and having now been left more than half-an-hour to myself in the schoolroom, I ventured to tap at the door and beg Miss Birch to let me into her room, as I would never, never, offend again.

"We will leave her to think over her disgrace and
shame, and let her beware of the birch again..."

After a very slight delay, the door was unlocked, and my governess received me with expressions of great tenderness, kissed her poor Lucille, and hoped my poor bottom was not too sore. Her eyes were melting with what I should now call a soft voluptuous languor, and scintillated with extraordinary brilliancy, all of which set my young ideas in a flutter of wonderment, as to the extraordinary cause of her prolonged emotion.

Things went on pretty smoothly for some time, but I found it quite impossible to avoid coming under the rod every now and then, the chastisement getting more severe on every fresh occasion.

Papa always had to handle the twigs, and when I began to get older, Miss Birch would tie me up and leave the room, as she pretended to be quite unable to bear the scene. Still papa would always go into her sanctum at the conclusion of my whipping, to talk the matter over with my governess.

I will tell you of a fearful birching, the last I had before being sent to the Convent School; it does not matter what the fault was, but it must have been something very serious. Papa and Miss Birch both helped to tie me up on a four-poster bed in my own room. I was stripped of everything but my skirts and drawers, which were all secured and arranged so as to expose my back parts in the best possible manner for whipping. My hands were tied to the bed post high above my head, and making me kneel on the bed, one leg was secured at the knee to the same post, my other leg being left free to kick about.

Miss Birch vanished, and papa arming himself with a formidable rood, elegantly trimmed as usual, began by lecturing me on my fault.

"You impudent girl, I can scarcely believe it of you, Lucille, now you are just upon twelve, but this is the last whipping you will get at my hands, and I promise you it shall be a sound one, and then I'll pack you off to the convent, with instructions to the sisters to be very strict in looking after you."

"Oh! Oh!! Papa," I implored, "Have mercy, don't be so severe, indeed I won't do it again!"

"Hold your tongue, Miss," he said, impatiently, "you always cry before you are hurt, but you shall remember this whipping as long as you live;" giving me a slashing cut round my loins, then another, and another on each cheek of my buttocks, "how do you like it, you bad girl! will you turn over a new leaf when you leave home? Will you? Will your? Will you? Will you?" Each question being accompanied by a terrific smarter; the blows seemed to cut like a red hot knife, and my boiling blood tingled from the tips of my fingers to the ends of my toes. I could feel great burning bursting weals rising on my skin at every cut; I screamed and plunged till the bed-post creaked with the strain, and my wrists and knee were quite pained by the tight ligatures by which they were secured.

"Let this be a solemn warning to you, Miss Lucille," he continued, "but I'm afraid all my efforts for your reformation are quite thrown away upon such a worthless baggage," cutting away still more furiously, and as I turned my head to scream and implore for mercy, I could see how excited he was over the business with flushed face and sparkling eyes; he was a fine handsome man of about forty-five, and gave me the idea of looking as if in the midst of a tremendous battle.

Anything but a bloodless battle for me; my bottom was soon dripping with the ruby drops of my young blood, the sight of which seemed only to exasperate him still more.

"Ah! You little wretch. Scream away!" he exclaimed. "It's a beautiful sight to see you writhing and plunging under every scathing cut. May it do you good and draw the imprudence out of your tail. Will you? Will you, try and behave better, or shall I send you off to the convent at once, in their holiday time? There! There!! There!!!"

He finished with three tremendous cuts, without waiting for my reply, and sank back, gasping for breath, into an easy chair. It was quite a minute or two before my screams and moans of agony subsided. Then Miss Birch coming in, released my hands and leg, an ordering me to rest on the bed for a while, retired with my father locking the door behind them.

The smarting sensation now turned to a delicious voluptuous warmth, as I lay under the bed clothes. My right hand was passed all over the glowing surface of my buttocks, and seemed at last, quite unwittingly to settle itself on my hairless little cunny. I turned on my belly with my hand still under me, and wriggling myself about, as I lay thinking over all the cuts I had received, gradually found a most pleasing sensation from the rubbing of my hand and the two forefingers mechanically worked into the slit, squeezing my legs together, I rubbed on to increase the pleasurable emotions which I felt driving me to strive and obtain, I knew not what. The frenzy now threw me into such a state of excitement that my fingers were plunged as far as possible up my virgin cunny, as I gasped, writhed, and tossed my bottom up and down. The crisis came at last, and my furious efforts were rewarded by a most heavenly emission; my soul seemed to flow from me at the moment, and left me in a delightful state of voluptuous lethargy, which lasted for some minutes, and when at length I regained my serenity, it was to find my fingers, cunny, and thighs all sticky from the thick spermy emission of my first maiden spend. There was also a slight stain of blood, for I had actually ravished myself in my furious excitement.

I got up and sponged myself, then lay down to reflect on the curious and delicious emotions I had procured for myself, and determining to soon have a repetition of my secrets joys, fell asleep to dream of being in the arms of a most lovely boy about my own age, who seemed to impart to my ravished senses another taste of what I had already felt.

Awaking in a struggle to retain my lovebird, I found myself bedewed by another emission, but at last I slept with tranquility, and never shall I forget my first taste of joy that day.

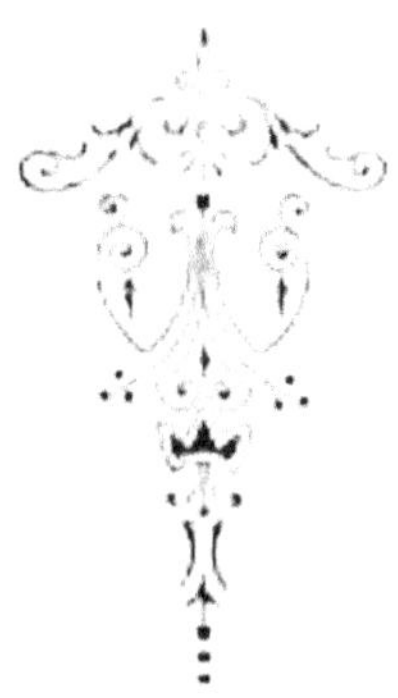

Chapter 11.

The Convent School

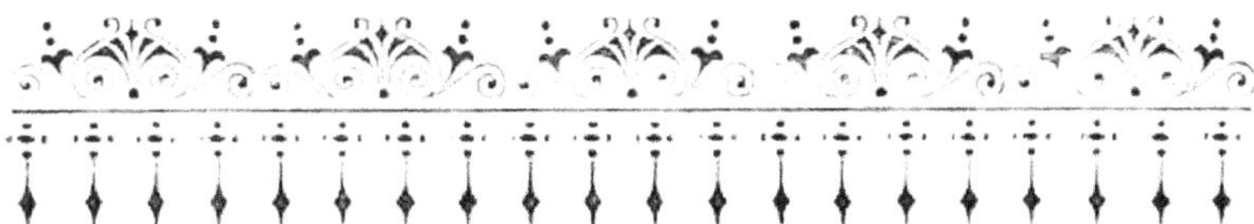

My father's extreme severity made me rather glad when in about a week's time Miss Birch began to make preparations for my departure to Belgium, and in less than three weeks I found myself installed as a pupil in the seminary of the Ursuline nuns at Brussels. The Lady Superior struck me from the very first as being a frightfully severe woman; the morning after my arrival she sent for me to hear her read my father's instructions and remarked that he had given her *carte blanche* as to punishment, and that in their school discipline was strictly enforced. "Remember, young lady," said she, in dismissing me from her presence, "we never overlook a fault, and that my word is law here."

My face flushed with indignation, and tears filled my eyes as I left the apartment, fully assured in my own mind that I must soon experience a taste of their discipline, nor had I long to wait, for two days after, having confidentially expressed my disgust to another pupil, with respect to the coarse fare set before us at meals, I soon found I had been talking to a tell-tale spy, who carried everything to the Superior.

An elderly nun quietly told me she had been sent to conduct me to the private room of the Lady Superior. My time had come, and I followed my chaperone with trembling anxiety.

Our Superior was a stern looking woman of about forty-five, with dark piercing eyes and Roman nose, thin compressed lips considerably adding to the severity of her expression.

"Mdlle. Lucille," said the superior, "I thought the caution I gave you on your arrival, would at least have saved you from trouble for some time, and spared me the pain of inflicting personal correction on you so soon after your entry into our seminary, but I am afraid your papa must have had serious cause for wishing me to be severe with you; now what have you been saying to your fellow pupil the Mdlle. Olive; did you remark, 'that the food was not fit for a dog, much less schoolgirls'?"

I looked down in confusion, "Ah, I see," she continued, "you cannot deny it; well Lucille, I hope soon to convince you that our bill of fare is both wholesome and proper for the pupils, I shall give you one dozen cuts with the rod, and then let you off if you promise not to offend in the same way again."

The nun who was called Serena, now placed a long stool in the middle of the apartment and made me lie on it full length face downwards, then I felt her cold busy hands as they turned up my clothes, and opened my drawers behind, till my bottom was left naked to the attack of the Lady Superior.

"Do you, Mdlle. Lucille," she asked sternly, "consider that our fare of bread and porridge three times a day, and meat or soup twice a week, added for dinner is only fit for a dog? Ah! Ha!" she went on, cutting me slowly and severely at every few words, "This will give you a better appetite; how do you like birch sauce, Miss Dainty Mouth?"

I screamed with the pain and plunged about so that Sister Serena had to hold me down with all her weight upon my shoulders. "Forgive me, oh, forgive me this time, I won't speak to Olive again!" I gasped out as the heavy woman almost stopped my breath, but at least it was over, and after kissing the rod and making me look at the blood-stained weals on my bottom, they

"This will give you a better appetite; how do you like
birch sauce, Miss Dainty Mouth?"

sent me away with a caution how I spoke about that or anything else I might see done in the convent.

I longed to have my revenge on the deceitful Olive, but knew not where to turn for a confidant, they all perhaps would be equally treacherous. I stuck to my lessons and avoided punishment as much as possible, being assured that the longer I brooded on my revenge the more complete it would be in the end, at the same time I thoroughly studied every part of the building to which I was allowed access, in the hope I might someday find it very useful if I wanted to affect my escape.

The nuns I believe slept in dormitories, where there were a dozen or more together, but every pupil had a very small room to herself, mine was in a long corridor, and Olive's three or four doors from mine, there were neither locks or bolts to any door, as the Lady Superior and elder sisters were supposed to take frequent peeps at us in our sleep; I had at last matured my plan, and having everything in readiness, one dark night when there was not even a glimpse of moonlight, I patiently watched till some of the principals had paid the accustomed visit, and heard the cracked voice of an old nun say, "fast asleep," as I feigned to be in a deep slumber.

Soon their footsteps died away in the corridor, and after waiting some time, till I felt sure every pupil must be again asleep, if the going round should have awakened them, I crept out of bed, and providing myself with some pins and a strong piece of cord, was soon at the bedside of the treacherous girl I wanted to serve out; my first act was to quietly pass my cord around her, outside the small bed, so that I could suddenly draw it tight and secure her a helpless victim in my power then suddenly stuffing the bedclothes into her mouth before she could scream out, ordered her in a rough whisper to keep quiet or I would kill her; it was too dark to see her terrified face, but she shuddered all over, and seemed as if her very blood was chilled, so cold did she seem to my touch.

Taking advantage of her fright, hands and feet were instantly tied so that she was spread out in a helpless fashion; I made her own handkerchief, which I happened to get hold of, into a gag, and at the same time could feel the drops of cold sweat upon her temples. Now I turned up the bedclothes or pushed them off, as I was tying the cord, till she was quite naked from the bosom downwards.

My hands roved over the soft, firm, naked flesh of her belly, then to the mount of love, which I found just beginning to be fledged with silky down. My fingers sought the crack below, and I could not help amusing myself by frigging her with all my might, the two first fingers of my right hand ruthlessly pushing into her cunny, and I knew caused her intense pain; from the slight groans which the gag could not entirely suppress.

What pleasure it was to me to torture her by my roughness, and outrage her every sense of modesty, although I was too ignorant at the time to know that my fingers were actually taking the poor girl's virginity; a kind of fury possessed me, and I actually bit the lips of her cunny, and munched off as much of the silky down as I could bite away; the pain must have been intense, and her writhing, shuddering agony was so much bliss to me.

At last to finish her off, I got a piece of the cord, and passing it right along her crack, tied it round her thighs and waist as tightly and painfully as possible, and then for ornament stuck a lot of pins in the plumb cheeks of her bottom and left them there.

My revenge was complete, so wiping my fingers on the bedclothes, for fear of any bloodstains, I left my victim just as she was, to be tormented by her horrible pains and fears till someone might find it out and release her in the morning.

This outrage was never discovered, my victim was found insensible next morning, and remained in a delirious state for three or four weeks before she recovered consciousness, and

"My hands roved over the soft, firm, naked flesh of her belly, then to the mount of love..."

then the agony and terror she had endured on that awful night had so turned her brain that she believed it was the devil who had so grossly ill-used her, but I heard that one of the father confessors was strongly suspected of having committed the atrocity.

The Superior, with whom Olive had been a favourite, now vented her spite in every direction amongst the young lady pupils of the seminary, and I for one soon fell under her displeasure, and was ordered to be tied up to their whipping post; it was only for slightly oversleeping myself, and not dressing quickly when the bell rang for us to get up at 6 a.m.

I was suspended by my wrists being tied high up the post as I stood upon a small footstool, then it was suddenly kicked away, the jerk of the sudden strain on my wrists almost making the straps cut into the flesh. My feet were dangling some inches from the ground, "Oh! Oh! Ah—r—r—r—re!" I screamed, "How cruel! Oh! Papa! Papa! If you only knew how they are treating me in this awful place!"

Lady Superior (who seemed delighted at the sight of my pain),—"Hold your foolish noise, Mdlle. Lucille, wait till you have something to scream about, girl." Then the old Serena, who it seemed was always in attendance at punishment time, pinned up my skirts and opened my drawers behind, and the Superior went on, "This rod shall make all the sluggards turn out quicker in the morning; what do you think, Mademoiselle, of making us all wait prayers for ten minutes? will you wake—wake—wake up sharper in future?"

She gave me three smarting cuts at each word, and my suspended position added so much to the intensity of my pain, that I screamed, kicked, and plunged about as I swung by my wrists from the post. "Sister Serena," exclaimed the Superior, "keep the girl steady or I cannot plant my cuts as effectually as I ought to do upon her naughty impudent bottom, she shan't sleep for a week if I can only make it sore enough!" Serena now held me to the post with one hand, to prevent my swaying about, whilst the rod rained a succession of withering, scorching cuts on my buttocks, and just underneath the parting of the cheeks of my bottom. My screams were heartrending, but they only seemed to enjoy it more and the Superior never ended her objurgations till the rod was worn out.

Things now went on till I was nearly fourteen, we never had a holiday, and only short letters came to me from home, in which my father constantly expressed his hopes of my improvement and seemed quite oblivious to all I had written from time to time about my severe treatment, and begging him to remove me to some other school.

I afterwards found out that my home letters were regularly suppressed, and others more suitable were written and sent to papa, in my name; what wretch that Superior now appears in my eyes, she not only delighted in whipping us nearly to death but forget letters to our parents so as to keep her pupils, and make everything appear *couleur de rose.*

Perhaps, dear Rosa, you have heard that I managed to escape from that dreadful convent, but previous to that they nearly killed me. I was getting quite a big girl, my pussey already sported its silken down on the Mons Veneris, which we all consider such an ornament to our secret charms.

The Superior had lately taken much notice of me, and introduced me to a clique of her favourites, three or four pretty girls about my own age, who were often indulged with little treats in her private room; there, we girls were encouraged and instructed in all kinds of lascivious ideas; we looked at each other's cunnies, tickled and kissed each other in every possible way, the Superior encouraging us, and suggesting a variety of attitudes for us to try. She had a huge godemiche, about nine inches long, and very thick, which she would fit upon one of the girls, and then submit herself to be fucked as hard as possible, whilst the other girls had to turn up the girl's skirts, and smack

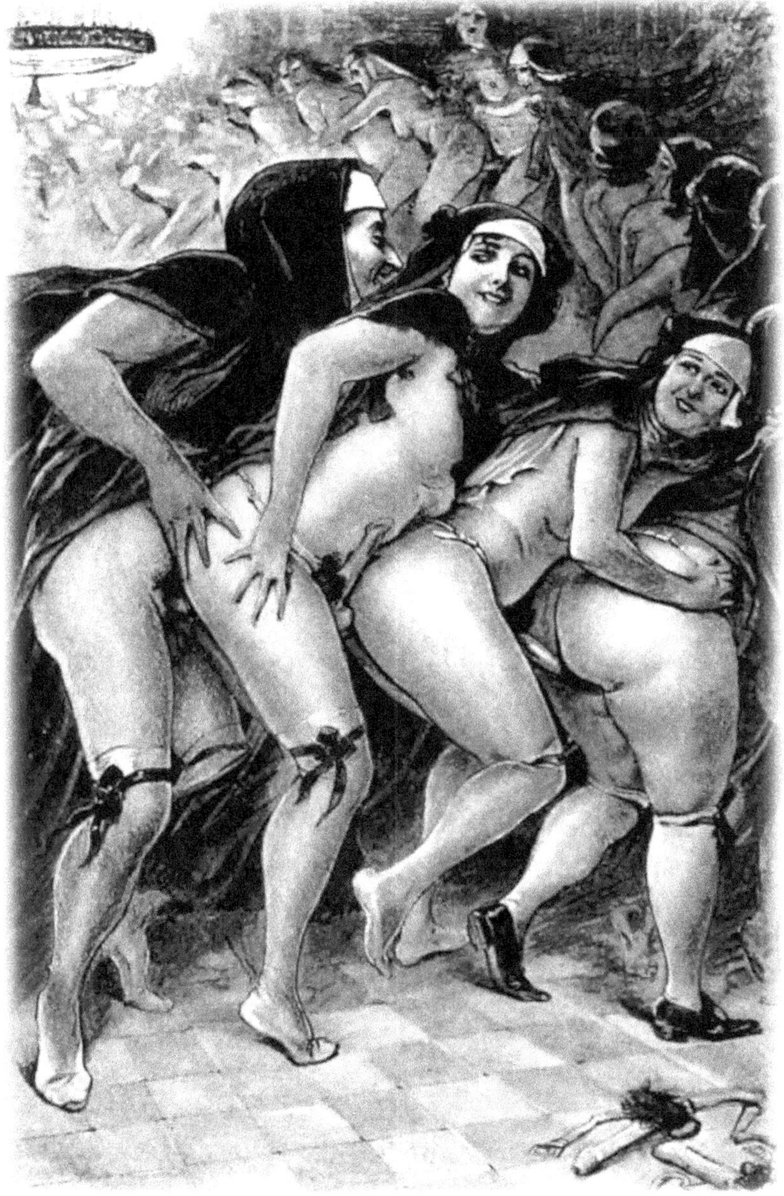

"...we girls were encouraged and instructed in all kinds
of lascivious ideas..."

her bottom hard and fast, with the palms of their hands, to make the young gentleman (as the Superior called her partner) work fast and vigorously.

Then she would have us all strip naked, whilst we had in turn to kiss and suck her cunt, when it was all slimy with her spendings.

I did not mind the slapping, or allowing any one to kiss and tongue-fuck my cunny, but the Superior's was so hairy, and had such meaty looking lips, and a huge clitoris, (which I now know is induced by long-continued self-abuse), and it smelt so fishy, that I absolutely declined the honour of gamahuching her, and nothing could induce me to do so.

This so enraged her that she flew at me like a tigress. I was knocked down, and beaten with a thick stick, till my flesh was bruised all over, and then picked up, almost fainting, and hurried off to my own little room.

Perhaps nothing further would have happened, but in my innocence, I supposed my letters were sent home just as I sealed them up, so I wrote to Miss Birch a full account of what I had been seduced into, and the dreadful beating I had received, for not liking the cunt of the Lady Superior.

The very next day after I thought the letter was gone, the old nun, Serena, fetched me into a dull gloomy room, which I had never been in before, but at once rightly judged to be a punishment chamber, when I saw a high whipping post, made of a square beam, set upright in the floor, with two rings near the top on each side, by which to tie up the victim; a birch rod was hanging on the wall, and two scourges with long things lay upon a seat at one end, but I had no time for further observation, as the Superior seemed to follow us into the room almost immediately.

"Now, Mdlle. Lucille," she exclaimed, grinding her teeth in rage, "you shall rue the insult you put upon me the other day, before my special favourites, of which I had minded to make

"What a beautiful position, how she will twist about and scream when she feels the scourge ..."

you one, so that when you left the seminary you might look back with pleasure to the loving amusements I had first introduced you to; perhaps I should have overlooked it all, but see I have your letter. Ha! Ha!! you little fool to think that would ever go out of the convent!"

Sister Serena had by this time put me on a stool and was fastening my wrists one on each side of the post, and presently the stool was removed, and I found myself just touching the floor with the tips of my toes.

"What a beautiful position, how she will twist about and scream when she feels the scourge, make haste to bare her bottom, as I am burning to pay her out. Ha! Ha!! Mdlle. Lucille, I fancy you wouldn't mind kissing my cunt now if I promised to let you off," said the Superior spitefully.

My courage and natural obstinacy came to my assistance at the moment, I was so indignant, and the idea was so repulsive to me that I resolved rather to die than do that for her; I was frightened and yet flushed with shame and indignation at my treatment, besides something seemed to advise me to irritate my tormentor to do her worst and get it over quickly.

"No! No!! No, never!!! you may kill me, and then I should be out of my misery!" I exclaimed.

She scowled with ferocity, but said with all the calmness she could command, "make haste, Serena, up with her clothes, and open the drawers well, and keep her as steady as possible." Then taking up the instrument of punishment I could see it consisted of five or six long thongs of whipcord, plaited and knotted at the ends, fixed on a very elastic handle.

It was poised in her hand for a moment, and then brought down with stinging force on my exposed buttocks, then again, and again, and again, in quick succession; each cut seemed to sear the flesh as if done by a red hot iron, my piercing screams filled the whole place, and the Superior, her eyes sparkling with ferocious joy, jeered me about how I liked the scourge. "How lovely you look, Mdlle. Lucille, as you plunge and scream, and I know the intense agony of every cut; would you rather die now, my little dear? Well, I've a good mind to kill you, outright, only I want to keep you as long as that *dear, kind papa* of yours is willing to pay! How he must have loved his Lucille, to place her with me; I'm so kind, so very kind, you know, my dear girl! What do you think of my kindness, you little love?"

Her cuts were awful, and I swayed and plunged so that it was impossible for Serena to keep my body steady, so she seized the other scourge, and tried her best to second the Superior in her efforts to cut me up more and more.

At last they fairly panted for breath, as I was left dangling, sobbing and moaning, with my clothes torn, my drawers in shreds, and streaming with blood all down my thighs and legs. Fearing I might faint, they poured a little strong cordial down my parched throat, sponged my face with cold water, and put some strong snuff up my nose, which almost drove me into convulsions, so very violent was the fit of sneezing produced.

They seemed carried away with delight at the sight of my sufferings and sprinkled a quantity of the snuff over the cuts on my bottom, just to dry up the blood, as they said with a laugh. Next all my clothes were cut or torn off, till I had nothing on but slippers, stockings, and the remains of my drawers.

"Now we'll finish off the obstinate, impudent little beast, I wish I dare kill her," said the Superior, grinding her teeth, "only I should lose too much, she is worth more alive than dead."

A couple of lady's riding whips were now produced, and the two women attacked me afresh; I was cut all over my body, each cut seemed as if done with a red-hot knife, the blood flowed down my back in streams, and yet their rage seemed to increase at the sight of my sufferings. My screams were awful, but only so much music to their ears. They jeered and derided my cries for "God to have mercy on me, &c.," said "my time was come to die, but they would make me last as long as possible and draw out my agony to the very last gasp."

This must all have passed in a very short time, but was an age of intense suffering to me, and the finale was such a display of ferocity that I sank under it, and thus robbed them of the pleasure of prolonging my torture. The Superior seized me by the hair, and drawing my head back, lashed her whip across my face and bosom, drawing more blood at every cut, whilst old Serena, not to be outdone, took my right leg under her arm, cut me dreadfully inside my thighs, along the crack of my pussey, and made the tip of her whip reach the Mons Veneris.

This was the last I could recollect, but when I came to myself, I was in my own bed, wrapped up in cloths soaked in water. No bones were broken, and my health soon recovered sufficiently to enable me to affect my escape, and avoid their further malice.

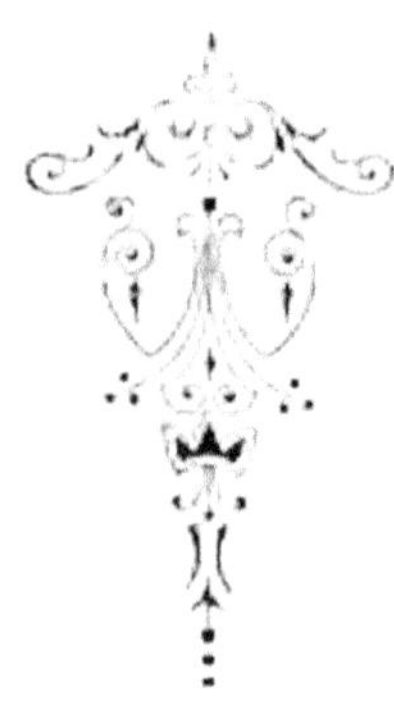

Chapter III.

Lucille's Marriage and Adventures

It was about 3 a.m. one fine morning when I escaped from the Ursuline Convent; and made my way to the Hotel d'Angleterre, the porter in answer to my summons was about to refuse to give me refuge, when a young Englishman, who was just taking his candle in the hall, said, "he'd be damned if I should not be taken care of," and ordered the chambermaid to be called to attend on me, and added that he would be responsible for all expenses. "Certainly, my lord," said the porter of the hotel, but he added *sotto voce*, "I think he's a fool to be so easily imposed upon."

I was too glad to have found a protector, (especially when I found he was an aristocrat), so I quietly followed the *femme de chambre*, and was content to await awhile for the *denouement* of my adventure.

Breakfast was brought to me about eleven o'clock, and also a message to say that Lord Dunwich, would do himself the pleasure of waiting upon me in an hour's time.

You may be sure I was all impatience to see the kind fellow who had stood my friend and was most agreeably surprised to find his manners quite equal to his appearance when I saw him again.

His Lordship was greatly interested by the account of my escape from the convent, and said he was a very particular friend of my betrothed husband, the Earl of Ellington, and would put me under the protection of a lady going to England, who would see me safe home. He was such a handsome fellow, and my gratitude was so gushing that at the moment I could have refused him no thing and was delighted by the way he lingered over a kiss, he would insist upon as his due, my whole soul seemed to leap towards the generous fellow, and tears of disappointment stood in my eyes when he was gone.

I never saw him again till my wedding day, two years later, when he was best man to my husband, and in my eyes looked a thousand times more loveable.

A married couple of sixteen and twenty-eight ought to have been blessed with every happiness, but after the first three days of our honeymoon the Earl's temper seemed so overbearing and imperious, that I began seriously to regret my fate, and looked forward to a life of gilded misery. The Earl was fond of the turf, and often left me alone 4whilst he spent a fortnight at Newmarket or Doncaster and York.

One day I was agreeably surprised by a call from Lord Dunwich, (we were living in Grosvenor Square at the time), he looked more handsome than ever, and seemed so full of sympathy for me in every respect that I could not help falling into tears, and telling him all my fears, and how I was neglected for nasty ugly fourlegged brutes of race-horses, and that in fact I was sure Lord Ellington loved his Derby favourite better than myself, and would rather I broke my neck than his pet should fall lame.

"Ah, Lucille" he said, falling on his knees before me, "how your distress cuts me to the quick, would to God, I could comfort you in any way! I have loved you from the first moment we met, although I knew you belonged to a bosom friend, and now the wretch slights you; look up, dear Lucille, from your tears, smile upon one who is devoted to your body and soul!" And then seizing my hand, upon which he imprinted a lot of

"Ah, you will pardon my presumptuous love,
how can I help it?"

impassioned kisses, "Ah, you will pardon my presumptuous love, how can I help it?"

I was piqued by the Earl's coldness towards me, and something impelled me to pity the handsome suitor at my feet, so that although the tears were still welling from my eyes, could not help smiling and caressing his head as he looked up to my face.

"Darling Lucille, I may call you so now, you respond to my love, my happiness is too great," he exclaimed, drawing my unresisting body down, so that our lips quickly met in a rapturous kiss of real love.

I was lost, and he so rapidly took advantage of everything, that proceeding from one liberty to another, in less than ten minutes I was an adulteress, but what a sweet sin, what transports of love shot through our souls as we melted away again and again in the ecstasies of mutual enjoyment; how we toyed with each other's most secret charms, and promised to renew our forbidden pleasure at every convenient opportunity.

Alas, for our happiness, some spy informed the Earl of my sweet *liaison*, he made an excuse to visit Brussels with me and again I found myself incarcerated in a hateful convent.
The kindness of my husband on our journey from England (which I afterwards found was only a part of his most artful programme), had so imposed upon my rather soft-hearted nature, that I really felt sorry that I ever been unfaithful to my marriage vows, although no doubt the image of my loving paramour was firmly imprinted in my heart.

We went to operas, bal masques, saw all the sights, and enjoyed ourselves immensely for a few days and being strict Catholics he one day said jestingly, "I suppose, Lucille, we must go to confession, and get absolution after having enjoyed ourselves, and confess all the delightful sins we have committed; by-the-bye, be sure you do not forget to confess having ridden a St. George on your husband, and allowed him to spend his seed in your hand, or on your pretty bosom, they are most awful sins, and will cost a pretty penny for absolution. I should not be surprised if the Rev. Father undertook to inflict personal chastisement *à la Girard et Cadière*," he added, laughing.

"But, seriously," I answered, "apart from joking, I know we ought to do it and will go to that church in the Rue de la Madeleine this very day, I know I am a sinner, but don't like to make a laugh of such serious things."

Then seating myself on his knee, I drew his face to mine, and kissed him lovingly, as I added, "But, dear Francis, you won't leave your little wife so long again, will you, for those horrid horses? You can't imagine how dull and low spirited I get when left all by myself."

"What a pretty pouting little bride you look. Why, Lucille, the way you kiss excites me as if we were still on the honeymoon trip; but dearest," he added, "a sporting man must see his horses tried and run, then, you, know, I shall make up in the winter what you lose in the summer; there's nothing else to do then but to make love. Ha, you sweet little devil, do you want to commit another sin before confession?"

My hand had been gently caressing his prick outside his breeches, till it was now rampant and impatient of the restraining cloth.

"Well," he went on, following my example, by passing a hand up my clothes, and gently tickling my clitoris with his forefinger, "we'll lump it all together, so there won't be any more to pay. My Stars, Lucille, how excitable you are. You're spending on my fingers. It's nothing to blush about, little simpleton."

I got off his lap, and kneeling before him, unbuttoned his flap, and the engine of love seemed to leap into my hand, its fiery head, with the skin turned back, looked so tempting, that I could not resist the temptation to kiss and caress it for a few moments. My tongue played lasciviously round the tender and

"I was lost, and he so rapidly took advantage of
everything, that proceeding from one liberty to
another, in less than ten minutes I was an
adulteress..."

excitable surface, whilst my hands, were fondling his finely developed balls.

"Darling! Darling!" he ejaculated. "It's coming! Oh! I can't stop—kiss—kiss—suck it. Take it in your mouth, Lucille! Oh! Ah! How delicious! You darling, to think you would give me so much pleasure!"

I was as excited as himself and sucked and swallowed his delicious spendings to the very last drop, as he pressed my head down with his hands, and gasped out his hands, and gasped out his ejaculations of ecstasy.

"Now, it's my turn, Sir. I mean to have a St. George, as you lie on the hearthrug. Come, down with you at once, or I will bite it off," making him feel my teeth, as I playfully took it again in my mouth.

We had a delightful bout on the hearthrug, and I rode him till he spent into my excited cunt a third time. Keeping his cock stiff, and starting him again after each spend by the contractions of the folds of my vagina, which he declared gave him the most exquisite and voluptuous sensations, and that he had never experienced anything to equal it in his life, many women as he had had in his time.

Presently I told him that as soon as I could get dressed, I would go to confession.

"Do love," he replied, "and if the Confessor is reasonable with you, I will go myself tomorrow or send for him to wait on me at the hotel."

I left him smoking a cigar, and about an hour-and-a-half afterwards entered the church, where I was immediately accosted by an elderly priest. "If the English lady wishes to confess, the Father Francisco in yonder box is most suitable for Madame. He knows the English ways so well and was consecrated in England."

I approached the box, which was in a very secluded corner of the sacred building, and kneeling on a hassock, enquired, in a low voice, "If the Rev. Father Francisco was ready to hear my confession?"

"Yes, my daughter, and I pray God you may have nothing but venial sins to confess," was the reply of my unseen Confessor.

In my innocence I related every act of our married life; how excited we were in our love games, and the various attitudes we used to heighten our enjoyment.

"Awfully sensual, my daughter. Your Confessor previous to marriage must have admonished you as to the use of these unnatural postures in following the dictates of nature in your endeavours to obey the first commandment, '*to increase and multiply.*' The holy rites of matrimony ought not to be perverted by lascivious ideas and filthy sacrifices to lust. It is a most serious thing my daughter, but before I consider what penance to exact for such sins, tell me, as you value the intercession of our Holy Mother, have you always been faithful to your husband? If only by a look or a gesture, it is important to your salvation hereafter that you should confess it now."

I was silent, dumbfounded for a moment or two. "Ah! my daughter, conceal nothing. Alas! it is as I feared—conceal nothing from me, or it will be impossible for me to grant you absolution." Thus pressed, and feeling but a full confession would avail me with the Confessor, I told him everything, and especially how sorry I felt at having allowed my pique at the Earl's neglect to have carried me into such a *liaison*, and that the tender regard he had lately exhibited towards me smote me to the quick for my unfaithfulness, and that that was the reason I had so given way to lasciviousness with him, in order to compensate, by the perfect abandon of my love, for any suspicions he might entertain.

"My daughter, I must consult our Superior. Yours is such a serious case, and I beg that you will go into the vestry, by the

"I found myself in the cell of a convent,
with the door locked behind me."

door behind this box, and wait a few minutes, till I bring you his decision," said Father Francisco.

I was all of a tremble, my face felt hot with blushes of shame, and I longed to hide from observation for a few minutes, so I readily went into the vestry, as he had requested. It was a bare scantily furnished room, with a few chairs, a writing table covered with papers, and some priests' frocks and vestments hanging round the walls.

Presently the old priest who had accosted me on my first entering the church, came to conduct me to Father Francisco's room, but instead of that, I found myself in the cell of a convent, with the door locked behind me.

The worst fears assailed my frightened mind; I sank on my knees, calling on God and my husband to release me, crying and stamping in impotent rage by turns; this must have lasted an hour or two. Then a little wicket was opened in the door, and the same old priest told me to calm myself, for Father Francisco and the Superior were praying to the Holy Mother to direct them what penance to impose upon such a sinner, and that I must remain where I was till next day, when, he added, "no doubt you will be restored to your loving husband, as pure in mind and spirit as when you first took your marriage vows."

I was going to implore him to allay the Earl's anxiety on my behalf, but he assured me they had sent to his lordship to say that I was doing penance for some hours in their convent, and quickly closed the *guichet,* so that I was again left alone.

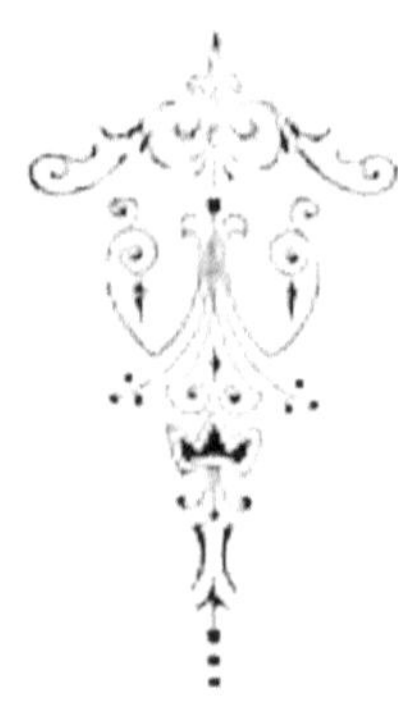

Chapter IV.

The Penance

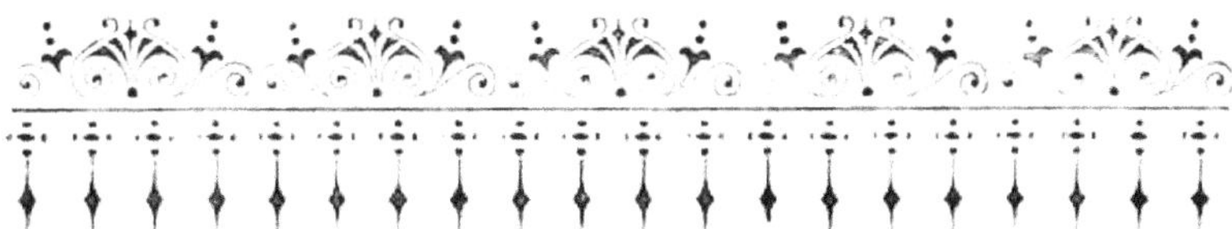

Two nuns supplied me with refreshment, made me up a bed on the floor, and I really had nothing to complain of as to treatment that first night, still, something seemed to assure me that I really was a prisoner, and should not so easily get out of the convent. My hope was, that the Earl would speedily insist upon my speedy release, (little dreaming at the moment that he was the instigator of my detention and had actually acted as confessor in the assumed name of Father Francisco.)

My anxiety was greatly increased the next day, when hour after hour passed, and still no communication from the Confessor or Superior, the nuns who brought me in breakfast and dinner were silent to all my enquiries or offers of bribes if they would help me get out of the place.

My watch had stopped for want of a key, but about seven o'clock in the evening, as near as I could guess, the old priest opened the door and beckoned me to follow him. My heart suddenly recovered its courage, and I braced up my nerves to bear the severest penance; we passed along several passages, and at last opening a door, he motioned me to enter. There, sitting before a small table, which had a bible and crucifix upon it, sat a rather young priest, about the same age as my husband, but with a close shaven face and crown (the Earl had heavy whiskers and moustache, I had never seen him otherwise), and he struck me as being very like Francis about the nose and eyes, still, no suspicion that it could really be him came into my mind.

"Daughter Lucille, Lady Ellington," said the seated Confessor, as the other locked the door behind me, "In answer to prayer, the Holy Mother has inspired us to grant you absolution, only after the most severe personal chastisement and humiliations we can possibly inflict upon you. Then, you will return to your confiding loving husband, purified of your adulterous sins, but for all that, he will still, and for the rest of his life, wear the horns of a cuckolded husband, which is his punishment for teaching you such lascivious ideas; it is an awful sin to so abandon yourselves to lust, and your unfaithfulness is the providential punishment he so well deserves."

My face and neck were suffused with the blushes of burning shame, as my eyes fell beneath his ardent gaze, besides something instinctively told me that both Father Francisco and his coadjutor were enjoying the sight of my confusion.

"Now please divest yourself of everything you have on, except corset, chemise and drawers, whilst I prepare this scourger for the chastisement of your wicked sensual flesh, and my brother here will get that rope in order, ready to tie up your hands above your head."

I scarcely knew how I got my dress and skirts off, as my hands trembled so, and the idea of stripping before two men, even if they were priests, was so distressing to my sense of modesty, but, somehow or other, I was soon standing up, with my skirts on the floor, about my heels, and my last under petticoat tucked up under my corset.

Father Francisco confronted me, scourge in hand, and pointing with his finger to my drawers in front, roughly ordered me to open them, and show where I had admitted my lover, when in the act of committing adultery.

"Open it, you wicked woman. I must see the seat of lust itself!"

"Open it, you wicked woman.
I must see the seat of lust itself!"

He flourished his scourge so, and gave me two such terrible cuts round my buttocks, that I was compelled to obey his immodest and shameful order, and the moment I had done so, he produced a pair of scissors and denuded me of nearly all the dark, silky chevelure I took such delight in viewing in the glass, whenever I dressed myself, or just got out of my morning bath.

"I suppose you were so excited and wanton, when Lord Dunwich embraced you, that you shewed him everything, even your nakedness, as the Bible calls it; did you blush then, as you pretend to do now, Lucille?" he asked.

My surprise and indignation almost choked me, so that I was unable to speak, and he gave me a heavy slap with his hand on my bottom, saying, "So you will not answer, and think I am behaving shamefully, do you? It's nothing to what you will have to submit to presently, Lady Ellington; turn round and open your legs, and stoop forward this instant, or I will flog the very life out of you!"

His rude hand was passed under my bottom, between my legs, and as I covered my face with my hands, I could feel his fingers invade every secret spot in turn, even to forcing a digit up the fundamental orifice, which is always so tight and difficult of entrance, saying, as he did so: "Did you let him go there, or has your husband ever sodomised your bum-hole? Ha! Ha! How modest we are now. Speak; say if you ever allowed any one to put his prick in your arse?"

I cannot recollect all he said or questioned me about, but his words and actions were every moment more and more coarse and obscene, on purpose to add to my humiliation.

"Here, Father Anthony," he continued, addressing the old priest, "where is your godemiche? That's the thing to draw all the wantonness out of her lustful body. It is well furnished with good stiff bristles?"

Father Anthony.—"It's a new one, same as we always keep in stock to subdue the fleshly lusts of these lascivious female sinners, and never used before, but I must tie her up."

The rope, which hung from a pulley in the ceiling, was tied tightly round my wrists, bringing both hands together; then he pulled it as hard as possible till I could barely touch the floor with my feet, and all my weight was upon my arms and the muscles of my back.

"That's it, exactly," chuckled Francisco. "Now, my dear Lucille, Lady Ellington I ought to say, you will really enjoy the insertion of this jolly dildoe up your cunt, and it is full of a delightful injection, with which it will spend in response to your emission of pleasure."

"Ah! No! No! Oh, pray don't treat me with such brutality," I screamed, in horror, when I saw the huge red-headed thing, with its shaft springing from a bed of bristles, fixed round the balls so as to prick the cunt at every insertion, besides its length and thickness seemed quite terrible to contemplate. "I am quite content to submit to your penance of scourging and whipping, but oh, oh, have mercy, and put that thing out of my sight."

Father Francisco.—"Look, you need not be so frightened. I shall lubricate it well with perfumed oil to make it enter you easily, besides I will put some on your cunt and bottom." Suiting his actions to his word, and oiling my privates profusely, especially my bottom-hole, which he lubricated till he could easily work two fingers in at once.

It was dreadfully disgusting, but still his frigging my bottom was rather exciting, and he could tell or guess my feelings, as he went on to say, "I see you like it, but the dildoe will make you plunge and spend with delight."

He then took up my legs; one under each arm, and stood between them, so they were wide apart, and Father Anthony, his face plainly showing how he delighted in the task, proceed to force his godemiche into me, opening the lips of my cunt with his fingers till the head was fairly in, then ruthlessly shove, shove, shove, till, "Ah! Ah! Oh! Ah—r—r—r—re!" I screamed in dreadful pain, as the sharp bristles ran into the tender surroundings of my pussey. "Ah! Ah! Oh, my God!" I screamed plunging and writhing in my agony, his eyes glared into mine with a fiendish delight, only equalled by the look of his companion, who held my legs like a vice, and encouraged him to fuck the wanton woman till she had had enough to keep her out of adultery for a long time to come.

Presently Father Francisco, digging his nails into the flesh of my legs, said excitedly, "See, see, she's coming. The gluey spend is glistening on your dildoe. Now, now, shoot it into her; let her enjoy it!"

In a moment I felt the hot gush of the contents of the godemiche. It rather relieved me for a moment or two, but oh, oh, my dear, even after this long lapse of time, I can never forget the agony of that moment. The whole of my body seemed filled with liquid fire, for they had filled the dildoe with some infernal decoction on purpose to ruin my health and destroy all chance of my ever enjoying the sweets of love again. Such I know was their intent, for they taunted me with it at the time; but although I never quite recovered from the shock to my system and feel even now that it was the original cause of my premature decay, they did not succeed in depriving me of all sensual desire or feelings for the future.

I fainted, but they never let me down, and when at last I began to recover consciousness Father Francisco was using his scourge most unmercifully on my buttocks, the drawers being open, and the naked flesh exposed to every cut.

"I thought this would bring her round", exclaimed he. "See, Father Anthony, her eyes are opening, it will soon make her forget the dildoe fucking, she did enjoy that, did she not, Anthony? But she'll be a long time before she has such pleasure again. Ha! Ha! Ha!!! how lovely she is getting, see her wriggle

"His rude hand was passed under my bottom,
between my legs,..."

from the pain of every cut. Ah, Lucille, dear Lady Ellington, what intense delight the sight of your agony is to us."

By this time either he was tired, or he thought a little respite would enable me to bear more presently, so dropping the scourge on the floor he left me still suspended, whilst himself and assistant sat down and gloated over the sight of my suspended figure and blood-stained bottom, with their hands under their frocks, and I verily believe now they were frigging themselves.

After about ten minutes Father Francisco again approached, scourge in hand, whilst the elder priest gave me a few drops of cordial and held some pungent salts under my nose to refresh me a little. "That will do," said the former, "stand back, Father Anthony. Now, now, you wicked, wanton, lustful young woman, did you wish your husband dead when having connexion with Lord Dunwich? Why don't you answer? Were his parts more pleasing to your sensuality? Is he better furnished than your husband? Speak up; confess all your wickedness! Did no sense of shame shock you in the midst of your enjoyment with that fellow, eh?"

Every question brought a scathing cut with it, breaking the weals and drawing fresh blood at every stroke, but I really was so ashamed I knew not how to answer, and my tongue was useless except for moans or cries of pain, and notwithstanding all their degrading and cruel treatment I felt it was fully deserved by me.

"Won't you speak? won't you confess your sorrow for your sin?" he continued. "Are you really so lost to all sense of shame as to be hardened against repentance? This must be whipped, yes, whipped out of you, even if it nearly costs your life!"

Just then Father Anthony loosed the rope a little, so that I could shrink further from the blows of the scourge, till I was driven up to the wall, where I stood on tiptoe with my hands drawn up over my head, and my back bending as much as

"Now, now, you wicked, wanton,
lustful young woman ..."

possible to avoid the terrible shower of blows with which he was cutting up my buttocks still more and more.

Crimson with shame, tears flowing in torrents from my starting eyes, I moaned, cried and implored for mercy, protesting in a broken voice, "That ever since my husband had renewed his kindness to me I had been very, very sad and ashamed of myself for what I had done, and only his former neglect had caused me to throw myself into the arms of a handsome man to whom I was under great obligations for protecting me when I escaped from the Ursuline Convent."

"Ha, then, you are that Lucille who insulted Lady Superior, I heard all about it at the time!" he went on furiously. "Now you shall be punished for that too," seizing my left leg and lifting it up, so that he could cut freely under my thighs, on my sore cunny, and every tenderest spot he could think of, whilst old Father Anthony was rubbing his hands in delight at the sight.

My agony was so intense that I could only gasp and sigh, strength I had none, he seemed beside himself with rage, but at last dropped his scourge, and throwing open his frock in front I could feel his rampant pego thrusting towards my mount, and am sure he spent on my drawers outside before he could get into me; this he soon effected, and taking my buttocks up in his strong embrace, he fucked furiously, swaying me about with my arms still tied up by the rope; but I forgot all that, his motions within me took away all feeling of pain, and I believe much as I loathed him and felt humiliated by all his dreadful treatment that I actually spent copiously when I felt his hot sperm shooting into and soothing my overheated cunt.

He was so overcome that Father Anthony seeing he was about to fall, released me, or loosened the rope so that we sank down together on the floor, and laid almost motionless for a few minutes, till the old priest, taking up a scourge, began to whip us both unmercifully, and made Francisco get up. This was the end for that time, but I was ordered to prepare for a final penance in a day or two's time.

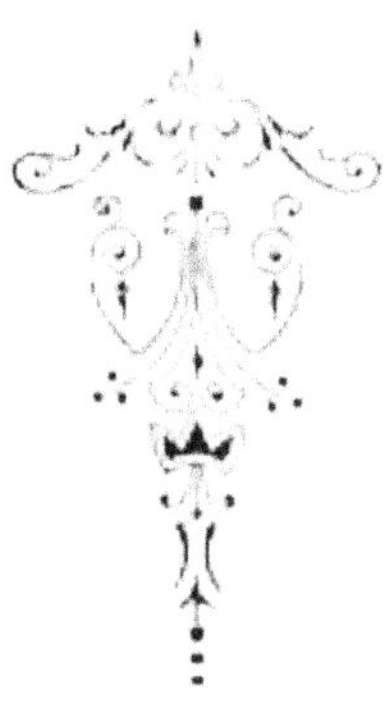

"...the two nuns nursing,—bathing my bruises, and using
soothing injections to allay the inflammations
of my privates..."

Chapter V.

The Last Scène and Denouement

They kept me in the same chamber, where I had been so outraged, the two nuns nursing,—bathing my bruises, and using soothing injections to allay the inflammations of my privates, till, on the third day, they said I was so far recovered that my Confessors might finish the prescribed penance, adding, with a malicious smile, "we saw everything last time, and so we shall now, through our peepholes; how delicious the sight was last time, and we had such frigging and dildoe fucks after it was all over."

Having said this, they speedily disappeared, and I was left to await my fate in trembling anxiety; I was hot and cold by turns, as the recollection of all the humiliating and painful incidents of the other day came back so vividly to my mind, and in imagination I seemed to suffer all my tortures over again.

This did not last long, although you may be sure it seemed long enough to me in my state of apprehension. A key was turned in the lock, and the door creaked on its hinges; my persecuting confessors again stood before me in reality, with quite a sardonic expression of anticipated pleasure on their faces; no trace of pity could I find on either visage, nothing but gloating sensuality seemed to animate the ardent looks with which they regarded me for some moments.

The hateful Francisco was the first to address me, a smile of terrible meaning playing round his mouth, showing his pearly white teeth to such perfection that I was again strongly reminded of my husband.

"Lady Ellington, I hope, has had good time for reflection upon the heinousness of her sins, particularly those in contravention of her marriage vows; wantonness is as nothing compared to that. What has the penitent Lucille to say? Has her chastisement made her feel the pangs of real remorse?" he said, whisking a scourge before my face.

I was too frightened to speak; face, neck and bosom, I could feel, were in a burning heat, whilst my eyes could not meet his, for something more than shame instinctively told me what I might have to suffer at his hands.

"No sign of repentance here, Father Anthony; she must be stripped naked at once. Do you hear, Lucille? Strip—strip—strip at once, or it will be much the worse for you!" he said with rough ferocity.

Both priests helped me to undress, and in their impetuous haste almost tore the clothes off my back, at the same time taking all sorts of disgusting liberties, and keeping me in a continued state of confusion, at last when nothing was left but my chemise to remove, they suddenly tied the rope round my left ancle, and in an instant I found myself suspended head downwards, with the right leg kicking in the air, and screaming piteously for mercy.

"Secure her wrists to the rings in the floor," said Francisco, "and then help me to whip the seat of lust till she is a little more repentant."

The elder priest speedily effected this, and then both of them with scourges commenced to whip me most mercilessly, aiming their relentless cuts between my legs so as to cut the lips of my cunt and round my bottom-hole at every blow; now and then the cruel thongs would wind round the upper part of my thighs, or on to my mount; my cries were heartrending, as each blow seemed to re-open all my old cuts and bruises. "Ah! Ah—

"...help me to whip the seat of lust
till she is a little more repentant ..."

r—r—re! Oh! Oh!! will you never have pity, and believe me sorry for my faults?" I screamed or moaned and gasped out the words in intense agony.

"So you begin to repent a little under the lash, do you, Lucille, are you really sorry for having wronged Lord Ellington, is it your mind or your cunt that is most filled with remorse? How you seem to writhe, and how prettily we are making it look for you, the trickling blood is delightful to see as it flows in drops and rills over your back and belly!" His questions were spoken slowly as he seemed to enjoy the pleasure of my intense suffering, and two or three of his cuts were over the tender surface of my belly or right across the navel.

"Scream away, you sensual woman, why don't you implore the Holy Virgin to have pity and forgive you, we are only carrying out her commands, are we not Father Francisco?" hissed out old Anthony, as he continued to scourge my back and sides, and every now and then aimed a fearful blow right down my lacerated cunny. Again, they would stop for a little, and ask me jeeringly, "about my feeling of remorse, would I indulge in such obscenity with my husband again, or keep from adultery in future?"

I was almost too far gone to do more than moan, and Father Anthony suggested that I ought to be well lashed over my neck, shoulders, and bosom, to make me speak out, but the other seeing how exhausted I really was, restrained his mad fury, and then after waiting a little one of them would give me a terrible cut, and ask the other to see the beautiful effects of it as I swayed about in agony; this was done again and again, till after a time the scourges were thrown aside, and the rope being lowered I was allowed to lay on the floor for a little while, and some cordial was again administered to refresh me, my tormentors sitting down and frigging themselves openly before my face, till in the act of spending they would stand over me so that I might be thoroughly humiliated by having all their spendings drop on my

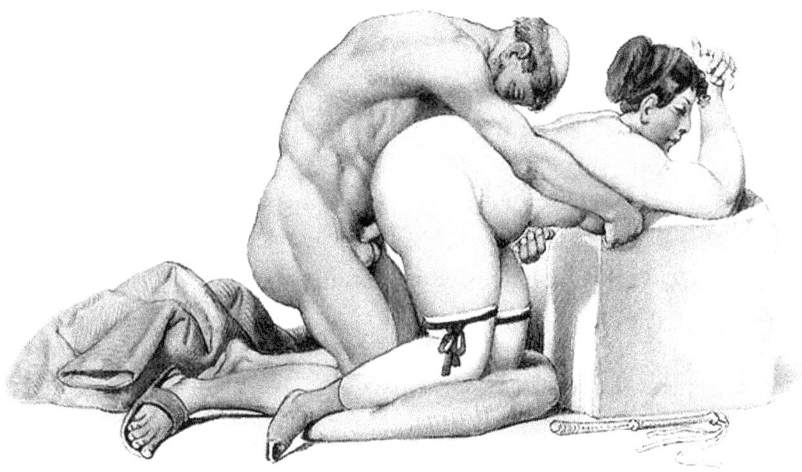

"Scream away, you sensual woman, why don't you
implore the Holy Virgin to have pity and forgive you ..."

face, neck, or head, as I was still secured to the floor by my wrists.

Presently, at a sign from Francisco, his companion hoisted me up by the ancle again, and did it so tightly that I was frightfully stretched by my arms and leg; which were drawn as painfully tight as he could make it, the fastenings cutting into the flesh so that I bear the marks to this very day, I could see that Francisco was again preparing his godemiche with oil, but he did not put any upon my person.

Horrified at the sight, I begged and implored them in the most piteous manner not to degrade me again with that disgusting instrument, promising to pay the Church any amount for absolution rather than endure it again.

"Too late, too late, your repentance is not sincere, besides, the other day we saw with our eyes how your lascivious nature responded to the thrusts of this thing in your cunt, now I am going to degrade your bottom-hole by inserting it there, however painful the operation may prove," saying which he seized, and held my left leg under his arm, and standing close to my body at once proceeded to carry out his infernal idea of ravishing my anus. Lacerated, bleeding, and sore as my bottom was at the least touch, and regardless of my piercing shrieks, he forced the oily head of the india rubber thing quite into my tightly contracted bum-hole, the pain was intense, as it seemed to rend the lining tissue of the anal canal in its passage, and the bristles round its root added, if possible, still more to the intensity of my suffering.

I believe, that giving one long shriek of agony, I lost consciousness for a time, but only to awake and find them laughing and jeering at my sufferings, as the one worked his dildoe in my bottom, whilst the other had thrust two or three fingers up my blood-stained and wounded cunt. It is quite indescribable what I felt at this outrage, the accumulation of shame, agony and horror so overpowered my exhausted nature, that I went off again into such a death-like swoon, that they really feared I was dead, and made haste to let me down as well as apply strong restoratives.

My hands were still retained in the rings on the floor, and the godemiche was left sticking in my bottom, the spasmodic contractions of the sphincter muscle holding it as in a vice, whilst the pulsations of the violated passage behind were still awfully painful. All this was apparent to me as I slowly came to myself once more and could see the excited looks of my cruel Confessors, who proceeded to sprinkle me with cold water, and use a large sponge for the purpose of both refreshing me and allowing them to gloat over the extent of my hurts.

This lasted a little while, then I was made to get up on my hands and knees, facing Francisco, who then opened his frock, so as to show me the excited state of his prick, at the same time, with a malicious look of fiendish joy, he asked me, "If I should not like to suck such a delightful sweetmeat?" Then seeing my look of intense disgust, he burst into a rage, saying, "Oh! So, you mean to insult me as you did the Lady Superior of the Ursulines, do you, Lucille? You may think I am disgusting and nasty, or I smell strong as she did, and I may tell you, to make you relish it still more, that scarcely an hour ago it was up the strong smelling cunt of that very same lady, and I was careful not to wash, so that you might have the full benefit of the delicious aroma of her spendings."

Speechless with disgust, and helpless in every way, it was useless for me to appeal for mercy or consideration from two such heartless beings; the only thing I could do was to close my eyes to the awful sight.

But only for a moment, a tremendous whack from Father Anthony, who had taken up the scourge, made me shriek out again, "Ah! Ah! Oh! Will you never finish me off, and kill me in mercy?" The only answer I had was a quick repetition of the blow, whilst the repulsive Francisco's right hand, clutching my hair, pulled my head up, and drew it back so painfully, that I

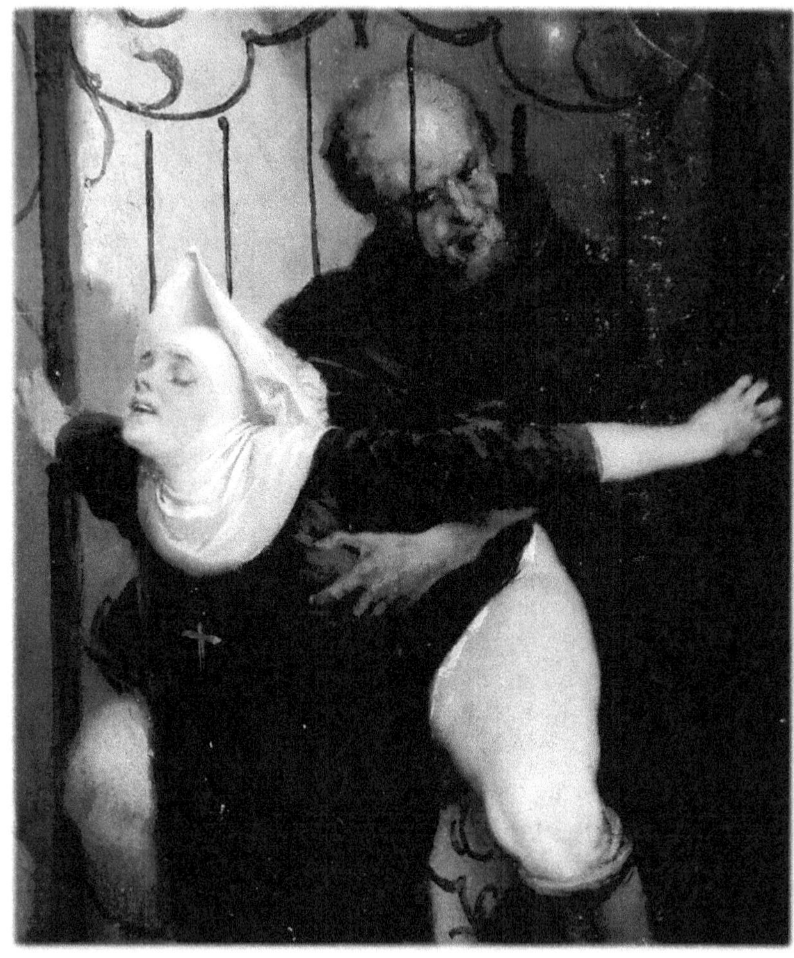

"...taking my buttocks up in his strong embrace,
he fucked furiously ..."

gasped for breath. This was exactly what he wanted, and, in a moment, his prick was forced into my mouth. The sensation was so repulsive, horrible, and choking all at once, that I had not the presence of mind to bite, or he would have repented the act ever after. Old Anthony was cutting my back, bottom, thighs, and loins, even the calves of my legs not escaping his frenzied scourging. Blood was streaming over my flesh, and dripping to the floor in little pools, and I felt I was really dying at last. Just then the excited Francisco shot a deluge of hot sperm into my mouth and throat; I was choked, and remember no more, except, that on recovering consciousness, the supposed Confessor, Francisco, was dressed as a gentleman, and I immediately recognised him as my husband, as, at the same instant, he exclaimed, "Woman, my revenge is complete. You won't deceive me again. How I have revelled in degrading, humiliating, and torturing my adulterous wife. You'll never see me more. This has been my way of divorcing myself from a faithless bitch."

He was gone before I could find words to reply, but my sense of pain was instantly drowned in a deep desire for vengeance for this outrage, and its impulse so strengthened me, that I was soon well enough to travel.

My lover, Lord Dunwich, received me with open arms, and declared he would shoot or be shot by the Earl ere forty-eight hours had elapsed; at once despatching a friend with his cartel to arrange a meeting for the next morning in Hyde Park at the dawn of day.

We spent the night together at his hotel, although scarcely fourteen days since I was so fearfully outraged, how we fucked all night, and swam in sensual pleasures for hours, I would deny him nothing, was he not my champion, who was going to risk his life in the morning to avenge my fearful wrongs, and to make him still more earnest in his desire for vengeance, I stripped naked, let him examine every part, where the marks of the

"Woman, my revenge is complete.
You won't deceive me again ..."

bruises and lacerations were still visible; my cunt he sucked, kissed and fucked till I was beside myself with excitement, and he was also ready for anything, then my poor bum-hole attracted his attention, he kissed and put his tongue into it, till I was eager to have him there, and begged he would put his prick in gently at first for fear of hurting me too much; this was a heavenly finish to our night of love; we swam in delight, never before or since have I tasted voluptuous joy to equal that *enculade.*

Next morning dressed as a young gentleman with a false moustache, I went as one of his seconds to the fatal place of meeting and had the satisfaction of seeing my wrongs avenged by a ball through the heart of my hated husband. We then went abroad for a while, but my dear lover lost his life by drowning in the Rhine, since which I have consoled myself as you know by all sorts of erotic fancies, especially flagellation, and now dear Rosa at the early age of twenty-five I find myself fast fading away.

FINIS

"I have consoled myself as you know by all sorts of erotic fancies, especially flagellation..."

List of Illustrations

www.ingramcontent.com/pod-product-compliance
Lightning Source LLC
Chambersburg PA
CBHW070344010826
48976CB00019B/2618